NOT A STICK

Antoinette Portis

HarperCollins*Publishers*

Gogh, Vincent van (1853–90). *The Starry Night.* 1889. Oil on canvas, 29 x 36¼
Acquired through the Lillie P. Bliss Bequest. (472.1941) The Museum of Modern Art, New York, NY, U.S.A.
Digital Image © The Museum of Modern Art/Licensed by SCALA/Art Resource, NY

Library of Congress Cataloging-in-Publication Data is available.
ISBN 978-0-06-112325-2 (trade bdg.)
ISBN 978-0-06-112326-9 (lib. bdg.)

Design by Antoinette Portis and Martha Rago
1 2 3 4 5 6 7 8 9 10
❖
First Edition

For Winston

Hey, be careful with that stick.

It's not a stick.

Look where you're going with that stick.

What stick?

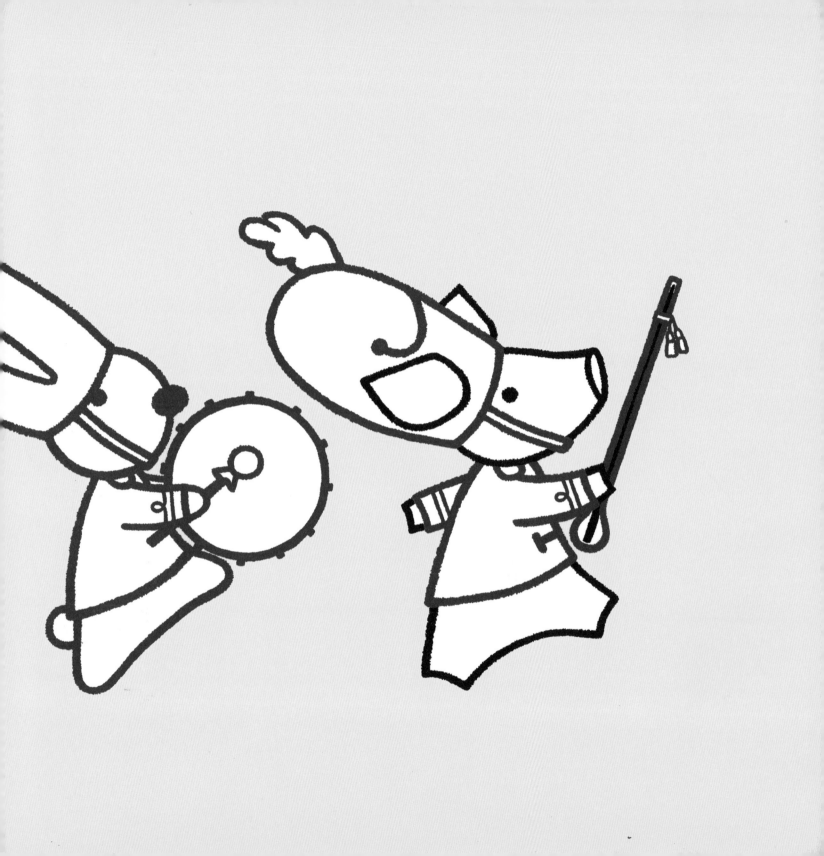

Watch where you point that stick.

This is not a stick.

Now what are you doing with that stick?

It's not a stick!

Don't trip on that stick.

I'm telling you, it's not a stick!

So, still standing around with that stick?

This is NOT NOT NOT a stick!

Okay. Then what is it?

It's my Not-a-Stick!